by
Jane Mason

SUPER HERO
SPLASH
DOWN

illustrated by
Art Baltazar

raintree

a Capstone company — publishers for children

Starring...

B'DG
THE GREEN LANTERN

DEX-STARR
THE RED LANTERN

SINESTRO DOG CORPS
THE YELLOW LANTERNS

ROLF

PRONTO

SNORRT

WHOOSH

GLOMULUS
THE ORANGE LANTERN

CONTENTS

Meet B'dg 4

Chapter 1
WATER PARK RIVALS 6

Chapter 2
SPACE CHASE 16

Chapter 3
FRIENDS AND ENEMIES 35

KNOW YOUR SUPER-PETS.................. 50
JOKES... 52
GLOSSARY.. 53
MEET THE AUTHOR AND ILLUSTRATOR.. 54

GREEN LANTERN CORPS
RING COMPUTER

B'DG Green Lantern, Sector 1014

Power Ring:
- creates anything imaginable
- flight
- force fields

HAL JORDAN

Green Lantern, Sector 2814

Species: H'lvenite

Place of birth: H'lven

Age: unknown

Favourite food: crisps and salsa dip

Bio: Like all members of the Green Lantern Corps, B'dg was chosen to protect an area of space from evil. He is pals with fellow Green Lantern Hal Jordan – not his pet!

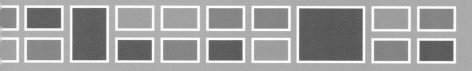

Chapter 1

WATER PARK RIVALS

"This is the life!" B'dg exclaimed.

The squirrel-like alien leaned back on his beach towel. He took a sip of his almond smoothie. **SLURP!** He was hanging out at one of his favourite places – the Waves O' Fun water park.

B'dg was a member of the Green Lantern Corps. He spent most of his time protecting outer space. Even with the help of his power ring, the task was not easy! He needed an afternoon off.

MUNCH! MUNCH!

B'dg nibbled on his straw. He took in the sights. All around him people laughed and enjoyed the sun. Kids splashed in the pools and sped down water slides. It was perfect.

Across the grassy lawn, people lined up to try to cross the lily pad path. But the lily pads were wobbly! Staying balanced was hard work.

SPA-LOOSH!

Children fell into the cool water.

"I think I'd better show them how it's done," B'dg said, getting to his feet.

He bounced across the lawn. Then suddenly, B'dg skidded to a stop. *No!* he thought. *It can't be him!*

Dex-Starr, a feline Red Lantern, sat at the edge of the pool. Red Lanterns got their power from anger. Dex-Starr was one grumpy kitty. Even at Waves O' Fun, he was scowling. His tail twitched angrily, making his power ring swing.

"Hello, Dex," B'dg said, running

over. "Are you enjoying the sunshine?"

Dex's tail twitched angrily again.

"You're not still cross about the

time I wrapped your tail around the

lifeguard's chair, are you?" B'dg asked.

B'dg gave Dex a little shove. The

super hero did not know his own

strength. Dex was thrown off balance.

He fell into the pool!

"**Whoops!**" B'dg said. He took a step

back to avoid getting splashed.

 Dex-Starr howled.

B'dg heard the Red Lantern's cries

before the cat's head broke the surface.

Dex yowled and pawed at the water.

"Want a paw?" B'dg asked.

Dex's eyes narrowed to slits. **He let out a long, low hiss.**

B'dg backed away slowly. When Dex stepped out of the water, he was soaked. With his fur all wet, the angry cat looked like a skinny skeleton.

"Check out the soaked kitty cat!" a boy called out, pointing.

"Looks like a wet rat!" cried another.

Several people started to laugh.  Dex cried. His tail flicked madly. Then a red beam of light shot out from his ring. It sizzled in the pool water.

He took a flying leap at B'dg. **The chase was on!**

Chapter 2

SPACE CHASE

B'dg leapt into the air. He landed on top of Toboggan Falls, a giant water slide. No sooner had he landed than Dex appeared behind him.

B'dg grabbed a raft from a lifeguard. **"Thanks!"** he called out. He hopped aboard and zoomed down the slide.

Dex's eyes burned with anger. He took a raft out of a little girl's hands. He followed after B'dg. **FWOOSH!**

Soon the rivals were neck and neck. Dex lashed out with a sharp claw. He poked a hole in B'dg's raft. **POP!**

BLUURRRP!

A second later, a balloon of air appeared all around him. It carried the Green Lantern back to the pool's edge.

"**Ha-ha!**" B'dg laughed.

"**You can't escape me!**" Dex shouted back at him.

B'dg skipped across the rubber rings floating along the nearby river of water. "Excuse me! Pardon me!" he told the park guests as he hopped over them.

"**Reeeoowww!**" Dex howled. The angry cat swished his tail. A red ray shot out of his ring.

The beam hit B'dg. It sent him flying through the air.

"Wee!" B'dg cried, enjoying the ride.

WHUMP! The Green Lantern

landed safely on the lily pad path.

Looking around, he smiled. *Now I*

can show these people what balance

looks like! he thought.

"Destroy his path!" Dex screamed

from behind.

BZZZZZT!

The lily pad floating in front of B'dg

exploded. Pieces of green plastic flew

in every direction.

"Hey!" a little boy cried. "That kitten blew up the lily pad!"

Thinking fast, B'dg leapt into the air. He pointed his ring at the empty space. He imagined a new lily pad in its place. In half a second, a glowing green pad appeared. **WOOOSH!** B'dg flew through the air, right over the deep pool. **"It's been fun, but I'm out of here!"** he called to Dex.

B'dg landed on the high dive. Then he took two giant jumps. He launched himself into the sky. **BOING!**

"**Hisssssssss!**" B'dg heard Dex's

cry of rage as he flew through a patch

of clouds. He did not look back.

B'dg focused on his ring and

imagined he was a rocket. Up, up,

up, he flew.

The alien squirrel soared away from Earth and into space. All around him stars twinkled and planets spun. A comet zoomed by as he got closer and closer to the Sun. It felt good to be out here again.

Then suddenly, B'dg felt something tug him from behind. YOINK!

The Green Lantern looked over his shoulder. He saw a red band of light beaming off Dex-Starr's tail. In another second, he would be pulled towards the evil cat.

Gosh! he thought. *Can't this kitty take a joke?*

B'dg had had enough. He did not want to fight Dex. The chase was not fun anymore. Enough was enough. He stared hard at his ring.

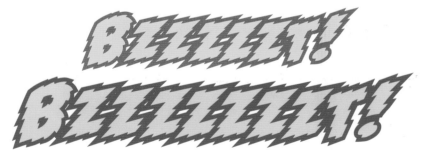 A ray of green light smashed against the ray of red.

The beams clashed against each other again and again.

29

"Ooof!" B'dg and Dex grunted with the effort. B'dg's arm began to tire. He got sweaty. The rivals were close to the Sun, and it was getting hot!

B'dg would not give up. "It was an accident!" he shouted at Dex.

The power ring rays clashed again, sending sparks flying. It looked like outer space fireworks!

Then suddenly, a chorus of barks came from behind.

Chapter 3

FRIENDS AND ENEMIES

B'dg looked around. The dogs were huddled together a few metres away. They argued over who should lead the way to Waves O' Fun.

"I'm the leader!" Rolf growled.

"Last time you led us to Earth we got lost!" Pronto shouted.

B'dg imagined a bunch of bones.

They appeared from his ring. He tossed

them into the doggie huddle.

ARF! ARF! ARF!

The dogs jumped on the snack.

Snarls and grunts could be heard

for kilometres. B'dg thought that the

snack would buy enough time to think

of a real plan. But five seconds later,

the dogs were already licking their lips.

**"Come on! Let's go and make

some waves!"** Rolf barked. He took

off towards Earth and Waves O' Fun.

"Thanks for the snack, pet!"

Snorrt called over his shoulder as the

pack of dogs took off.

"I am not a pet!"

B'dg shouted. **"I'm a Green Lantern!"**

"Reowww!" Dex chased after them.

The evil cat's red beam shot through the blackness of space. His anger made the beam grow longer and longer. Soon, it was in front of the pack of nasty dogs.

Dex swung his tail. He made his red ray zigzag across the galaxy. **"Here, doggies,"** he said.

Rolf began to follow the lights. The pack of Sinestro Dogs followed.

"Lead them to Nupe!" B'dg said.

Nupe was a tiny moon close to the Sun. It had strong gravity. If they could get the dogs close enough, they would get stuck there like magnets.

Dex-Starr swung his tail in a giant arc. He turned the dogs away from Earth and towards Nupe.

The dogs howled as they followed the red light. Suddenly, they stopped.

"Rolf, you're getting us lost again!" Pronto growled.

The dogs were on to them! B'dg stared down at his ring. He imagined that he was in a kitchen filled with roasting meat. He focused on the smell and put it into his ring. Then he flew right into Dex's red beam and sprinkled the delicious odour out in front of the dogs.

The dogs' noses twitched in the air.

"Roast meat!" B'dg whispered to the hounds.

"My meat!" Pronto cried, taking off after the smell.

"Mine! Mine!" the others barked.

The smell of the meat got stronger and stronger. Soon the dogs were racing towards Nupe.

"My meat! No! Mine!" they shouted. B'dg flung that last bit of roasted meat odour at the dogs. He grinned as they got caught in Nupe's gravity.

They were stuck in an invisible net.

Dex-Starr chuckled to himself. He
pulled the red beam back into his ring.

"Dex, did I just hear you laugh?"
B'dg asked.

Dex narrowed his yellow eyes. **"Of
course not,"** he said. His tail twitched.

B'dg smiled. The pesky Sinestro Dogs would not be causing trouble for a while. And Dex-Starr was not angry with him – at least not at the moment.

"Waves O' Fun, here we come," B'dg called. He and Dex took off towards Earth. **"I can show you how to cross the lily pads."**

"You mean I can show *you* how to cross the lily pads," Dex meowed.

They soared past planets and stars and through Earth's atmosphere.

Soon they were zooming through puffy white clouds and touching down at Waves O' Fun.

When his paws hit the ground, B'dg could tell that something was wrong. Nobody was in the water. Lifeguards were blowing their whistles. People were running and shrieking. And there was a strange orange glow coming from one of the pools.

B'dg scanned the lily pads and saw the problem.

Glomulus, the disgusting Orange Lantern, was sitting in a lily pad next to a giant heap of junk food.

"Where'd he come from?" B'dg said, pointing at the orange blob gobbling hot dogs and slurping sodas.

BLURRRRP!

Glomulus let out a loud burp.

"If it's not one Corps, it's another!" Dex said. **"Those greedy Orange Lanterns ruin everyone else's fun."**

"They really do," B'dg said. He knew Glomulus would be hard to get rid of.

"Oh dear," B'dg said to Dex-Starr. **"Suddenly, the Sinestro Dogs don't seem so bad."**

THE END

KNOW YOUR

Krypto

Streaky

Beppo

Comet

Ace

Jumpa

Whatzit

B'dg

Storm

Topo

Ark

Hoppy

Paw Pooch

Bull Dog

Chameleon
Collie

Hot Dog

These are
**HERO
PETS.**

Tail Terrier

Tusky
Husky

SUPER-PETS

Ignatius

Chauncey

Crackers

Giggles

Artie Puffin

Griff

Waddles

Rozz

Dex-Starr

Glomulus

Misty

Sneezers

Whoosh

Pronto

Snorrt

Rolf

Squealer

Kajunn

These are **VILLAIN PETS.**

JOKES

Why did the cat run from the tree?

Why?

It was afraid of the bark!

How do you catch a space squirrel?

Dunno.

Climb a tree and act NUTS!

What is a cat's favourite sport?

Tell me.

Hairball!

GLOSSARY

balance ability to keep steady and not fall over

distract weaken a person's focus on someone or something

focused concentrated on someone or something

gravity force that pulls things down towards the surface of a planet

imagined pictured something in your mind

rival someone you are competing against

MEET THE AUTHOR

Jane Mason

Jane Mason is no super hero, but having three kids sometimes makes her wish she had superpowers. Jane has written children's books for more than 15 years and hopes to continue doing so for 50 more. She lives with her husband, three children, their dog, and a gecko.

MEET THE ILLUSTRATOR

Eisner Award-winner Art Baltazar

Art Baltazar defines cartoons and comics not only as a style of art, but as a way of life. Art is the creative force behind *The New York Times* best-selling, Eisner Award-winning, DC Comics series Tiny Titans and the co-writer for *Billy Batson and the Magic of SHAZAM!* Art draws comics and never has to leave the house. He lives with his lovely wife, Rose, big boy Sonny, little boy Gordon, and little girl Audrey.

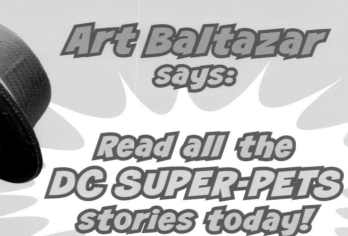

Raintree is an imprint of Capstone Global Library Limited, a company incorporated in England and Wales having its registered office at 264 Banbury Road, Oxford, OX2 7DY – Registered company number: 6695582

www.raintree.co.uk
myorders@raintree.co.uk

First published by Picture Window Books in 2011
First published in the United Kingdom in 2012
The moral rights of the proprietor have been asserted.

Art Director and Designer: Bob Lentz
Editors: Donald Lemke and Vaarunika Dharmapala
Production Specialist: Michelle Biedscheid
Creative Director: Heather Kindseth
Editorial Director: Michael Dahl

ISBN 978 1 4747 6444 5 (paperback)
21 20 19 18 17
10 9 8 7 6 5 4 3 2 1

British Library Cataloguing in Publication Data
A full catalogue record for this book is available from the British Library.

Printed and bound in India